昨晚我帶月亮去漫步，
她好像一隻夏日風箏在後面與我同路，

Though there wasn't a string or a tail in sight
when I took the Moon for a walk.

當我帶月亮去漫步時，
我看不見有鳶綫在尾部。

I carried my blue torch just in case
the Moon got scared and hid his face.

我會帶著藍色的手電筒，
以防月亮害怕，藏起她的面孔。

當我帶月亮去漫步時，
她卻從輕紗般的雲彩後偷看。

But it peeked through clouds
that were fragile as lace
when I took the Moon for a walk.

I warned the Moon to rise a bit higher
so it wouldn't get hooked on a church's tall spire,

我忠告月亮升高一點，
免致她被教堂的尖塔鈎著，

While the neighbourhood dogs made a train-whistle choir when I took the Moon for a walk.

當附近的狗群合唱出火車汽笛般的曲調時，
我帶月亮去漫步。

We tiptoed through grass where the night crawlers creep
when the rust-bellied robins have all gone to sleep,

我們踮著腳尖悄悄地走過爬蟲夜行的草叢，
紅衣知更鳥都早已熟睡，

當我帶月亮去漫步時，
月亮喚出露水，露珠猶如眼淚一樣滴在綠草上。

And the Moon called the dew so the grass seemed to weep
When I took the Moon for a walk.

我們跑去盪鞦韆，
讓雙腳踢得高高，
想像月亮要與我一起飛翔，

We raced for the swings,
where I kicked my feet high
And imagined the Moon had
just asked me to fly,

Hand holding hand through the starry night sky
when I took the Moon for a walk.

手牽著手越過星光燦爛的晚空。
我帶月亮去漫步。

We danced 'cross the bridge where the smooth waters flow.
The Moon was above and the Moon was below,

我們跳著舞，走過橋，平靜的河水飄流在下面，
月亮在上空，月亮也在下面，

我在她們之間回應著她們的光芒。
我帶月亮去漫步。

And bright in between them
I echoed in their glow
When I took the Moon for a walk.

Then as we turned back, the Moon kept me in sight.
It followed me home and stayed there all night,

當我們調頭回家時，月亮一直照耀著我，
隨著我回家，徹夜伴著我，

And thanked me by sharing its sweet sleepy light
when I took the Moon for a walk.

用她使我甜蜜安睡的柔光感謝我。
我帶月亮去漫步。

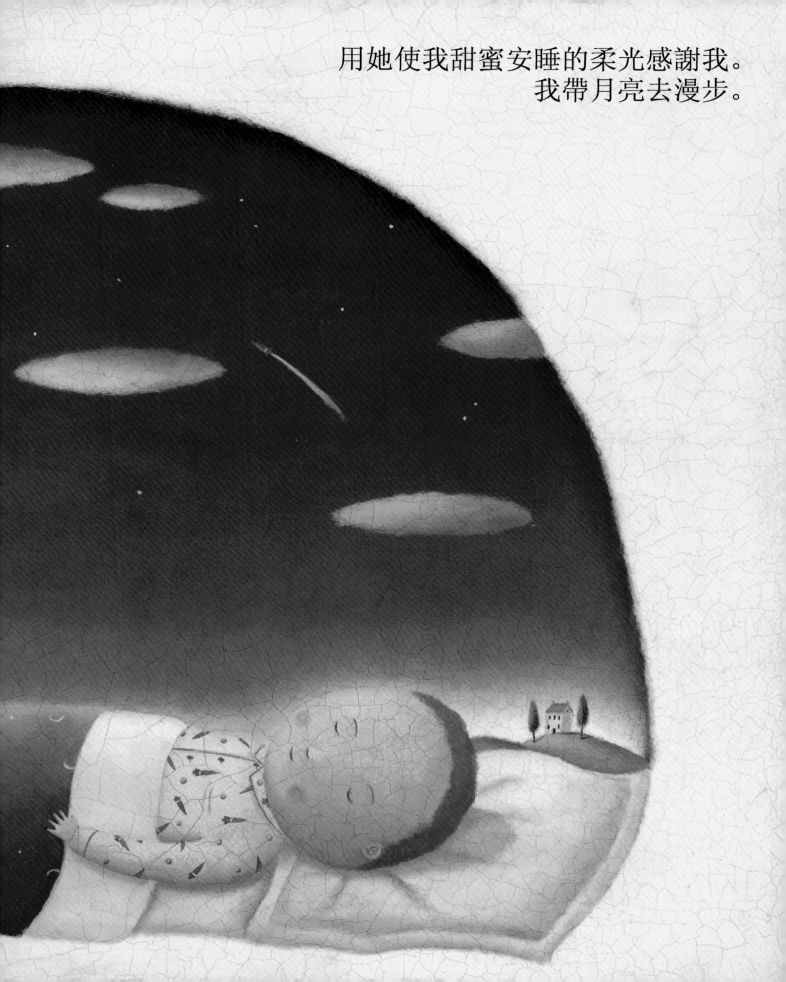

The Mysterious Moon

What do you see when you look at the moon? Children who live in Europe and the United States imagine that they see a man when they look at the moon. Children in Japan and India see a rabbit, and children in Australia see a kitten. But all children, no matter where they live, look up in wonder at the same moon.

The moon is primarily made of rock with a small iron core. It creates no light of its own, but reflects sunlight.

The shape of the moon seems to change during the month because the sunlight strikes the moon at different angles as it travels through space. These shapes are called 'phases'. Here are some of the phases of the moon:

New Moon   Crescent Moon   Half Moon   Gibbous Moon   Full Moon

When the moon is growing larger in the sky, we say that it is 'waxing'. When it is growing smaller, we say that it is 'waning'.

For people all over the world, the moon has always been an important way to measure time. Although the solar calendar has become the standard international way of doing this, many people still use lunar, or moon, calendars.

The moon can be a friend to farmers and gardeners - those who follow tradition know that the best time to sow seeds and transplant young shoots is when the moon is waxing.

Moon festivals are celebrated in many societies. The Chinese Moon Festival is held during the Harvest Moon - the full moon that rises in mid-autumn.

Many Celtic and Native American festivals are also held at the time of the Harvest Moon, when the people give thanks for the harvest and for all living things on earth.

The World at Night

If you took the moon for a walk through your neighbourhood, what would you show it? What would you hear, and what would you see?

Wherever you are, you would probably see some nocturnal creatures - mammals, birds and insects that usually sleep during the day and come out at night. They are especially adapted to life under the moon and stars:

Cats have eyes that see very well in the dark.

Rabbits have large ears that capture sound across long distances.

Bats use sounds and echoes to help them fly safely and find food.

Fireflies light up at night so that they can find each other.

Owls have necks that can turn right around and huge, flat eyes that enable them to see other creatures that are far away.

Some flowers are nocturnal too. They bloom and release their fragrance after dark.

And although you are asleep during the night, your mind is not! During the day, your waking, or conscious, mind is active, but when you sleep, your dreaming, or unconscious, mind is busy. So, the world at night is not so quiet as it seems!

For my nephew Christopher, *who first walked with the moon*
and my mother Estella, *who held his hand*
For my father Harold, *the star we steer by*
and Lucan, *my sun*
and, of course, for Emilie, *for Everything* - C.C.

The author extends heartfelt thanks to the society of Children's Book Writers and Illustrators for generous support in the form of
a Barbara Karlin Grant, WarmLines Parent Resources, Jane Yolen, the Jeff Kelly and Newton Library Critique Groups, and Alison Keehn.

For Mark, happy moon walking, love from Alison.

Mantra Lingua TalkingPEN
Global House
303 Ballards Lane
London N12 8NP
www.mantralingua.com
www.talkingpen.co.uk

First published in Great Britain in 2004 by Barefoot Books Ltd
Dual language edition first published 2008 by Mantra Lingua
This edition 2012